ORPS

BEAR COMPANY

CAMERON ALEXANDER

BICKERING
OWLS
PUBLISHING

This one is for my boys

Dark Corps series. Bear Company
by Cameron Alexander
Published by Bickering Owls Publishing

Copyright: Cameron Alexander
Illustrations: ©Bickering Owls Publishing

Cover Art and Book Design by Rhett Pennell

ISBN: 978-0-9991138-1-3

First Printing July 2017

CONTENTS

CHAPTER 1:

THE SECRET BASEMENT

There is a place, a place unlike any place you've ever been to, a place at the top of the world that is frozen and isolated, which means there is nothing around it at all—unless you count ice as something, and in that case, there is a lot of something around it. If you were standing in this place, all you would see around you for miles is white and blue; white, because of the miles and miles of flat, frozen land, and blue, because of the cloudless sky above you.

But if you squinted very hard you might see something far, far off in the distance. This something would look very small and square and black. And if you wanted to know what that something was, and if you dared to walk for miles across the flat, frozen land you would eventually see that it was a very small building, no larger than a garden shed, perfectly square and made of black bricks that shimmered in the sunlight.

There would be a door on this small, square building, but no doorknob. But if you were particularly clever and managed to get inside, you would probably be surprised to see that this building wasn't a building at all, but an elevator that leads down, under the flat, frozen wasteland and deep underground to an undisclosed research laboratory—undisclosed being a fancy way to say that it's so top-secret that no one talks about it, not ever.

And if you walked across all those miles of frozen land and got to the small shed-sized building and got inside and took that elevator down underground, and if you weren't yet surprised because maybe you lead a very exciting life and this sort of thing happens to you all the time, well... now you would definitely be surprised, because you would discover that this underground facility is where all of the most secret, sensitive, and classified experiments are carried out.

If you've ever heard of Area 51, which is a place in the Nevada desert that, according to some people, is where the government keeps the bodies of aliens that crashed here on Earth, you would very soon see that this underground base under the frozen tundra of this undisclosed location makes Area 51 look like a candy shop.

And finally, if you managed to wander far enough in this underground base under the frozen tundra of this undisclosed location and you weren't arrested by government agents and carried away to a room where they erase your memory so you can't recall what you've seen, you might find a long, wide room with bright fluorescent lights overhead, just like the ones in schools, and inside this room you would find Dr. Peter Barnes, a world-famous scientist who works here—but not at all by choice.

* * *

The intercom crackled and a harsh male voice barked, "Mr. Barnes! Report!"

"Doctor," sighed Dr. Barnes. "It's Doctor Barnes." Dr. Peter Barnes was known all over the world for his many scientific achievements and discoveries. He had traveled across every continent; he had spoken at the very best universities; he had cured disease and found evidence of life on other worlds.

But thirty days ago he was tricked into coming here to this secret basement a half-mile under the surface of the earth. The agents had told him it was a once-in-a-lifetime chance to do something truly extraordinary—and they weren't lying about that. No, instead they lied and told him that he could leave whenever he wanted, but once he was down here, he found it to be quite the opposite. He was locked in this room and was not allowed to leave until his experiment was successful.

"Mr. Barnes!" the harsh voice barked again.

"Report!"

Dr. Barnes pressed the small black button next to the speaker and said loudly, "It's Doctor Barnes, if you please. And I have told you a thousand times, the experiment is not ready!"

"You're taking too long," the voice grumbled.

"The machine needs to be perfectly calibrated," Dr. Barnes explained. Building the portal was not terribly difficult, at least not for him, but his calibration—which means small changes and adjustments to make something just right—was the hardest part of the experiment. "If everything isn't exactly right, we don't know what will come through the other side."

The voice on the intercom was silent for a long time. Then finally it said, "We expect a test in one hour."

"One hour?" Dr. Barnes exclaimed. "You

can't do that! It's far too soon—"

"We've given you plenty of time," the voice said. "One hour." Then the intercom fell silent and stayed that way.

Dr. Barnes drew in a long breath and then let out a deep sigh. About a year ago, he had made an incredible scientific discovery—he had used math to prove that there were other dimensions, which means other worlds that exist at the same time and place as ours, but worlds we cannot see or touch or feel. It's like if you took a sheet of paper and folded it in half. If you drew a stick figure on one half, and another stick figure on the other half, the two stick figures would exist at the same time and in the same place, but not together.

Of course, that's a very simple way to put it, but Dr. Barnes used very complex math to prove that his theory was correct. And then, a month ago, two men in black suits came to his office with their offer of a once-in-a-lifetime chance to do something amazing—which, he later learned, was to build a portal, or a doorway, between our world and another.

The problem, as Dr. Barnes was very much aware, is that we have no idea what's on the other side.

CHAPTER 2:

THE LONELY BOY

Timmy Barnes was a very lonely boy. While most ten-year-old boys went to school and played sports and video games and made friends, Timmy stayed indoors and did his schoolwork in his bedroom.

It wasn't that Timmy wasn't nice, or fun, or smart—in fact, he was all of those things. No, the problem was that Timmy's dad was a famous scientist, and because of that they moved around very often. Sometimes they only stayed in one place for a few months, and then they packed up and moved again. They never really stayed anywhere long enough for Timmy to make friends, and after a while of moving around so much, Timmy stopped trying.

There was nothing in the world that Timmy loved more than having his dad around. When Dad was home, he would show his son things like how to throw a curveball or how to make a campfire without any matches. He would teach Timmy the names of the stars and they would go on long hikes and talk about everything and anything they could think of. Because they moved so many times, Timmy had seen much more of the world than most people do in their whole lives, and his dad would take him to exciting places like ancient ruins and space shuttle launches and rivers where the water flows upstream.

Unfortunately for Timmy, his father wasn't around very much. He worked long hours, and sometimes he was gone for days at a time. While his father was gone, Timmy found himself very lonely. He was afraid to try and make friends because he knew he would have to leave them soon, so instead he stayed in his room and he worked on the schoolwork that his father had left for him. He read science-fiction books and dreamed of space battles and befriending aliens and finding new, exotic species of wildlife.

But mostly, he would stare out the window at the small park across the street and watch the kids play basketball and freeze tag.

While his father was gone for work, Timmy was left in the care of a nanny. He could remember the names of all eleven nannies he'd had since he was six years old. His father would go through a lot of trouble to make sure that the nanny was warm, kind, and took very good care of Timmy—which is why Ms. Gertrude was so strange.

Ms. Gertrude wasn't just a strange nanny; she was a strange woman. For example, she always wore a business suit of black slacks, a black blazer, and a crisp white shirt. Her hair was always in a very tight bun on her head. Her nose was sharp and a little crooked, as if it had been broken before and didn't quite heal right.

But most importantly, Ms. Gertrude didn't seem to like children very much.

Three times a day—at breakfast, lunch, and dinner—she would call up the stairs very loudly, "Timothy! It is time to eat." Timmy would come downstairs and they would sit together at the dining room table and eat in silence. Ms.

Gertrude was always reading something, either the newspaper or sheets of paper from a manila folder.

At some point, usually about halfway through the meal, she would suddenly say, "Timothy, have you finished your schoolwork?"

To which Timmy would reply, "Almost."

Then Ms. Gertrude would say, "Good," and that's all she would say.

He hated being called Timothy.

Even though Timmy was used to his dad being away at work, this time was definitely the worst—and not just because of Ms. Gertrude. His father had been away for a whole month now, and he had not called or sent an email or even a letter, not once.

Every now and then Timmy would ask Ms. Gertrude, "When's my dad coming home?"

Ms. Gertrude would sigh, as if the very

idea of Timmy wanting to know anything was annoying to her. She would glance down her sharp, crooked nose at Timmy and tell him, "When he's finished."

Timmy was a lonely boy, but he wasn't completely alone. Before his dad had left a month earlier, he gave Timmy a gift. In fact, he gave Timmy a gift each time they moved in the last four years. The very first time, when Timmy was only six and his mother had just passed away, they moved to an old farmhouse near a river, and one morning his dad put a tall white box on the kitchen table.

"What is it?" Timmy asked.

"You won't know until you open it and see," his father replied.

Inside the box was a stuffed lion. It was about two feet tall, and since Timmy was only six and still very short, the lion reached his waist.

"His name is Leo," his father told him, "and he'll protect you while we're here."

Timmy gave the lion a hug and was surprised at how soft and fuzzy it was—that is, until he noticed that there was something hard and rigid behind it. He turned it over and saw that Leo was wearing a square metal case on his back.

"What's this for?" Timmy asked.

His father smiled. "Don't you worry about that."

After a while they moved out of the farmhouse by the river and into a log cabin in the middle of a forest. As they were unpacking their things, Timmy noticed that Leo was missing.

"I'm sorry, Timmy," his father said. "I guess Leo had to stay behind. But don't worry; I have something else for you." And he put another white box on the table, a bigger one this time. Inside were four plush wolves, each one as soft as a pillow, and each one also with a hard metal case on its back.

"Is that where the batteries go?" Timmy asked.

His dad laughed and said, "These toys don't take batteries. But don't worry about that. These wolves will protect you while we're here. And this time, you have a whole pack of wolves! That's what a group of wolves is called—a pack."

And so it went: each time they moved, some stuffed toys would be left behind, but there were always new ones. Sometimes they were farm animals; sometimes they were forest critters; sometimes they were jungle mammals or desert reptiles.

As Timmy got older, he stopped playing with the stuffed toys, but he didn't want to tell his dad that. Instead he took the gift and said "thank you," because it was something to remember his dad by when he was away at work.

On this last move, the day before his dad left for a month, there was a new white box on the kitchen table.

"What is it?" Timmy asked, like he always did.

"You won't know until you open it and see," his father said.

Inside the box were five stuffed bears, each one softer than the last, and each one with a hard metal case on its back. Even though all five bears looked the same, they were all different colors. There was a red one, a blue one, an orange one, a yellow one, and a green one. Timmy had no idea why he needed five bears, instead of just one, but he didn't ask. He smiled and said "thank you" and brought the bears upstairs to his room, where he stuck them on a shelf side by side.

Every day, while he did his schoolwork or watched the kids across the street play in the park, Timmy could look over at the bears up on the shelf and remember that no matter where his dad was, or what he was doing, he was thinking about him.

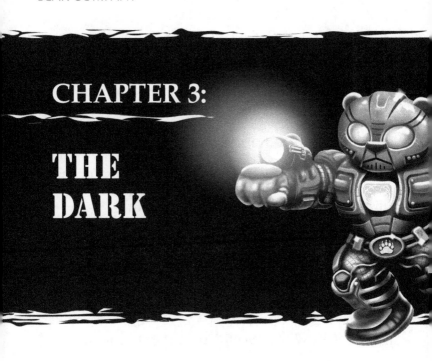

CHAPTER 3:

THE DARK

"**I** have to get to Timmy!" Dr. Barnes said out loud, even though there was no one else in his big white room in the underground lab. "Keeping him safe is the most important thing in the world right now!"

If anyone had been watching Dr. Barnes at that moment, it would look like he had gone crazy, because not only was he talking to himself, but he was talking into an air vent. But what no one else knew was that he was *not* alone, and that someone was listening, inside the air vent.

"Stick to the escape plan," Dr. Barnes told the vent. "We have no idea what's coming through the portal. If it's what I think it is…"

The voice on the intercom had given Dr. Barnes one hour until he had to open the portal, and that was fifty-seven minutes ago. Any moment now, he would be expected to turn on his machine—and no matter what happened he would try to make his escape from this place.

There was only one door in or out of the room, and it locked from the outside. Dr. Barnes heard a *ka-chink* as someone on the other side unlocked it. A moment later, the door opened and six people came in, three men and three women. They were all dressed the same way— black pants and a black blazer with a crisp white shirt. They all wore dark sunglasses over their eyes, which made them all look like twins to Dr. Barnes (actually, they would be called "sextuplets." Twins are two people that look the same; sextuplets are six people that look the same.)

"Dr. Barnes," said one of the agents, "it is time to test the machine."

"Please," Dr. Barnes said, "I beg you. Do not turn on this machine. We don't know what's on the other side."

"We've waited long enough," said one of the female agents.

"Too long," said another. "If you ever want to go home and see your son again, you will turn on that machine."

Dr. Barnes sighed. "Okay. Come with me." He led the six agents to the other side of the wide room, where there was another doorway—but it did not lead in or out. This doorway stood by itself, just a frame with three sides and no door in the center of it. The outside of it was made of sturdy metal rods with hundreds of brightly colored wires snaked all around them, and a long antenna at the top.

"This is the portal," Dr. Barnes explained. "When I turn it on, and if it works, it will open a doorway between our world and another world."

"It's not very pretty," said one of the male agents.

"Sorry, I was a bit rushed," Dr. Barnes replied, annoyed. He went to a computer on a desk nearby and quickly typed in a command: OPEN. But before he pressed the enter key, he looked back at the agents. "Are you sure you want to do this?"

One of the agents looked at her watch. "Let's hurry this up, doctor. You're not the only top-secret experiment going on down here, you know."

The male agent next to her held up a sign that said "WELCOME ALIENS!"

"Okay. Here we go." Dr. Barnes pressed enter on the computer, and then he pulled a pair of heavy black goggles over his head to protect his eyes.

Sparks of blue electricity popped and crackled from the corners of the doorway. For a moment, it didn't look like the portal would work—in fact, it seemed like it was broken. As sparks flew from the many wires coiled around it, the white fluorescent lights overhead dimmed until the room was almost entirely dark.

Then, suddenly, a bright blue light filled the doorway, so bright that the agents had to look away, even in their sunglasses. Only Dr. Barnes, with his heavy black goggles, could look right at it. The doctor held his breath. The portal was open; the blue light was the door between our world and another. But who, or what, would come through?

The answer, it seemed, was nothing. The blue light began to fade, and soon the doorway was just as dark as the rest of the room.

No—it wasn't *as* dark. It was darker.

"It didn't work!" one of the female agents cried. "You failed, Dr. Barnes!"

But the doctor ignored her. He was too busy examining the doorway. He lifted the goggles to his forehead and looked closer at the portal. The doorway was still there—but it was as black as ink. He couldn't see through it.

"How very strange," Dr. Barnes mumbled. He reached for a screwdriver and very carefully poked the inky black doorway. As soon as the tip of the screwdriver touched the portal, it was quickly sucked inside with a sound like *schloop!*

"Oh my!" one of the agents gasped.

"What is it?" another asked quietly.

"We need to close this." Dr. Barnes hurried to his computer to enter the CLOSE command.

He only typed C-L-O before one of the agents behind him shouted, "What's it doing?!"

The inky black surface of the portal bubbled out and into the room, so big that it threatened to pop—and then it did. With a sound like a car backfiring, the black bubble exploded, and hundreds of shadowy shapes spilled out across the floor, up the walls, over the ceiling.

The agents ducked and covered their heads as shadows flew all around them, over them, filling the wide, dark room and making it much, much darker.

"We need to get out of here!" one of the agents shouted, but his friends already thought of that. In just a few seconds, the only one left in the room was Dr. Barnes and hundreds of shadowy shapes.

The noise was incredible—it sounded like a hundred voices were all talking at once in hissing whispers, as if they were trying to force a breath out and talk at the same time.

But Dr. Barnes was a man of science, and men of science are not easily frightened. Instead of typing the CLOSE command, he instead typed DESTRUCT and pressed enter.

Yellow sparks popped from the portal, and the inky black doorway vanished. At least that was one problem solved. Of course, there was still the problem of hundreds of black shadow-creatures surrounding him.

He stood up straight and tall and said very loudly, "My name is Dr. Peter Barnes. Who are you, and where do you come from?"

Suddenly all of the hissing voices fell silent. The shadows did not have eyes, but Dr. Barnes felt as if they were all looking right at him. He couldn't see them very well in the dark room, but he could see that the shadows were not very large—not much bigger than an average-sized dog, actually. Some of them were in the shapes of beasts, casting shadows of horns and teeth. Others were in the shapes of small humans with too many or too few arms and legs. Others were simply inky black puddles on the floor and walls.

Then one shadow rose up, right in front of him. It was taller than the doctor, the four points of its shadowy spiky horns reaching the ceiling. It had no arms or legs, but just a column of shadow and four large horns.

"Tell me, Dr. Barnes, are you afraid of the Dark?" the shadow asked. Its voice was by far the most horrible; it sounded like a cross between

a dog's growl and a car driving on gravel.

But Dr. Barnes was not afraid of the dark, and hadn't been since he was a little boy, so he stood up tall and held his head high and said, "No. I'm not afraid of the dark."

"*You will be*," said the tall shadow.

Dr. Barnes stared at the shadow as he secretly reached one hand behind his back and felt for the computer keyboard. He was very good at typing, but he had never tried to type anything backwards and without looking.

Very carefully, and so the shadow wouldn't see, he pressed eight keys: A-C-T-I-V-A-T-E. Then he pressed enter.

CHAPTER 4:

BEAR COMPANY, ACTIVATE!

*"**H**eek!"*

Timmy awoke in the middle of the night and sat up. It took him a minute to remember that he was in his bed, in the house in the city. He was cold and a little frightened. He'd had a bad dream. In his dream, he was running away from something that he couldn't see—there was only a shadow, always behind him and getting closer.

He could have sworn that he heard a noise, and that the noise woke him up, but it must have been his imagination.

"It was just a dream," he said out loud, because sometimes saying things out loud helps to believe it. "All just a dream!" He even laughed a little bit, feeling silly.

"*Heek!*"

Timmy froze, his eyes open wide. That time he *definitely* heard a noise. He looked around in the darkness, but all he could see were the familiar shapes of his desk and his dresser and his toy chest.

"*Shh!*"

Timmy gulped. Someone else was in his bedroom. He dared himself to get out of bed and turn on the light switch, but his legs did not want to move.

"Is someone there?" he whispered. He

was surprised at how tiny his voice sounded. He stayed quiet for a long time, just listening. Several minutes went by; there was not a single sound in his room.

Finally his legs decided to work again. Very slowly, he got up from bed and went to the light switch on the wall and turned it on. The sudden brightness hurt his eyes, but he forced himself to look. There was no one else in his room—at least not that he could see.

He checked under the bed. There was nothing there.

He looked in his closet. Nothing there either.

"*Heek!*"

Timmy gasped when the sound came again. It sounded like half-hiccup, half-sneeze… and he was almost certain that it had come from the other side of the room. But that couldn't be; the only thing over there was his shelf and the five plush bears his father had given him.

He tiptoed over to the shelf and squinted his eyes so he wouldn't have to blink, in case any of them made the noise again. He glanced from one bear to the next. They were as silent and lifeless as they had always been.

Finally, he looked over the red bear. He would never say it out loud, but the red bear was his favorite. Somehow it always felt warm when he touched it, and sometimes, when no one else was around, he would give the red bear a hug because he liked feeling the familiar warmth of it.

Timmy stared at the red bear for a long time, and then—even though he felt really foolish—he asked out loud, "Did you make that noise?"

Of course the red bear didn't answer his question.

Instead she said, "Don't be afraid."

"GAH!" Timmy cried out. He was so startled that he fell backwards, tripped on a remote control truck, and landed flat on his back on the carpet.

The red bear had talked. It had moved its mouth and *talked* to him. And now, as he watched, the red bear stood up, stretched its stubby legs, and hopped down from the shelf, landing softly on its plush butt.

Timmy very much wanted to get up and run away, but his legs decided not to work again so he laid there on the floor, breathing hard as the red bear held out both her paws and said, "Timmy, please don't be afraid. We're friends."

Timmy pinched his arm very hard. "Ow!"

"Why did you do that?" the red bear asked.

"Because you're a bear! And a toy! Toy bears don't talk or walk!" Timmy was almost shouting.

"Please, be quiet or you'll wake the nanny," the red bear said. "You're right. I am a toy, and I am a bear… but I'm also a lot more than that. I know this is hard to understand. I promise, I'll explain everything. But right now, we have to go."

"Go?" Timmy asked, confused. "Go where?" He wasn't sure he wanted to go anywhere with walking, talking toys.

But the red bear didn't answer his question. Instead she looked up at the shelf with her fellow bears and said, "Bear Company, fall in!"

The green bear stood first, a fierce grin on his face. "Finally, we get to see some action!" He jumped down from the shelf and tumbled onto the carpet.

"Try not to hurt yourself already, Bruiser," said the yellow bear as she hopped down to join the green and red ones. Next came the blue bear, and finally, the orange bear, who landed on the carpet with a thud and a "*Heek!*"

"You were the one making that noise?" Timmy said.

"Yeah, what's going on with you, Squeak?" said the green bear.

"My name is not *Squeak*," the orange bear said. "It's Sneak. And I don't know what's wrong with me." Sneak rubbed a paw over his round plush belly. "Something's not working right."

"Not working right?" Timmy repeated. "What do you mean?"

The red bear came closer. Timmy wanted to scramble away, but then she put her paw on his arm. It felt warm and fuzzy, like it always did, and it calmed him a little.

"Listen, Timmy. It's dangerous for us to stay here, but I can see that you need to know what's going on," she said softly. "Your father built us.

We're not just toys or gifts; we're more than that."

"Are you… alive?" Timmy asked.

The red bear shrugged. "In a way. Do you know what 'artificial intelligence' means?"

"No… wait, sort of." Timmy remembered that on one of their hikes, his dad talked about artificial intelligence. "It means that you're a robot that can think for itself, right?"

The red bear smiled. "I don't think we like to be called robots. But yes, we can think and we can learn and we can do all sorts of things. Now, your father activated us—that means he turned us on from wherever he is—and we have only one goal, which is to keep you safe."

"Safe from what?" Timmy asked, suddenly feeling colder.

"We don't know yet," the red bear said. "All we know is that your dad built us to protect you, and to take you to a meeting place where he can pick you up safely."

"Excuse me, I don't mean to be rude," Timmy said, "but how are five stuffed bears going to protect me from anything?"

The red bear chuckled. "We'll show you. Bear Company—suit up!" As soon as she said that, there was a whirring noise, and the metal case on her back opened up. Plates of armor slid over her plushy arms and legs and belly, and in only a few seconds the bear was covered from head to toe in shining red armor. Each of her paws now ended in four robotic fingers; even her soft, fuzzy ears were now protected behind metal, and the round lenses over her eyes glowed red.

"Wow," Timmy whispered. As he watched, the other four bears did the same, and in moments five armored bears stood before him, suddenly looking less cute and cuddly and much fiercer than stuffed animals.

He couldn't believe his eyes.

"Is that better?" the red bear asked him.

"Um… yes." Timmy nodded. He wiggled his toes to make sure his legs were working again, and then he stood up. He knew he was about four feet and six inches tall, and the bears didn't even reach his waist—they were only about two feet tall each—but with their shining armor and matching-colored blazing eyes, he was sure they could protect him just fine (assuming, of course, that they were friendly).

"What do I call you?" Timmy asked the red bear. "Do you have a name?"

"A name," she repeated thoughtfully. "I have a codename that your dad gave me when he built us. My codename is Mother."

"Mother?" Timmy said in surprise. That was

a very odd name to give a bear. Unless…

See, Timmy was a smart boy. He was smart enough to know he was not dreaming, and he was smart enough to know what artificial intelligence was. He was also smart enough to know that if his father had named the bear Mother, then it was a secret code to Timmy to let him know that he should go with her.

"Okay… Mother," Timmy said after a minute of thinking. "I'll come with you. But where are we going?"

"We need weapons," said the green bear.

"Yes," said Mother, "but first we need to leave here. Whatever threat we're facing might be on its way here now. Bear Company—let's move out!"

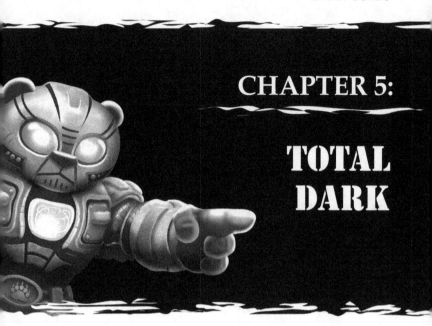

CHAPTER 5:

TOTAL DARK

Dr. Barnes sat at his desk chair, like the tall shadow had asked him, and tried not to move much. The shadow with the four horns glided back and forth across the wide room, as if it was waiting for something.

It had sent the other shadows out into the underground lab, and now the only ones in the lab were him and the doctor.

"I told you my name," Dr. Barnes said. "What do I call you?"

"*You may call me Total Dark*," said the shadow in its horrible gravelly voice.

"Okay then, Mr. Total Dark. Where do you come from?" the doctor asked.

"*We come from a world of shadow and darkness*," said Total Dark.

Dr. Barnes nodded. "I see. And what exactly is your plan here?"

"*We will take control here, and then your entire world!*" the shadow hissed.

The doctor looked at his wristwatch and said, "Hm."

Total Dark stopped pacing and turned toward him. "*What? What is it?*"

"Well, it's nighttime now. But on Earth, we have this thing called a day, which is when a giant light in the sky—that's called the sun—comes out and makes everything bright. I'm no expert, but I would guess that your minions won't like that very much."

Total Dark let out a low growl. "*Then we will travel only at night, or in the shadows.*"

"Sure," said the doctor.

"*Be silent now, human. My minions should return any moment.*"

Dr. Barnes was quiet for a little while, but as a scientist, he had a lot of questions. "So your plan is to take over the whole Earth, huh?"

Total Dark growled again, as if he was annoyed. "*Yes. What of it?*"

"Well… Earth is kind of a big planet. There are billions of people here, and I only saw a few hundred of your shadow critters come through." Dr. Barnes shrugged. "I don't think you're going to be able to take over the planet with just a few hundred shadows."

Total Dark was silent for a full minute. "*Billions, you say? That's a lot of people.*"

"I know," the doctor agreed. "It boggles the mind."

"*Aha!*" Total Dark said suddenly. "*I have a solution. You will open the portal again and let more of my minions through. Thousands of them! Millions, if necessary!*"

"Gee, Mr. Dark, I'd love to help you… but I already sent the self-destruct command," Dr. Barnes told him, trying to look very disappointed. "The portal is broken."

"*I demand that you fix it immediately!*" Total Dark screeched.

"I'll try, but I can't make any promises." Dr. Barnes turned his chair towards the computer and typed in a new command, F-L-A-S-H-E-R-S, and then the enter key. "Nope, sorry, it doesn't look like I can fix it."

"*You're trying to trick me,*" Total Dark said.

"I wouldn't do that," Dr. Barnes insisted.

"*I can smell fear, Doctor. And right now, you're afraid that I'll see through your deceit.*"

"I would say I'm more nervous than afraid," said Dr. Barnes.

"*Let me show you what else I can do.*" A wisp of black shadow, like a very thin arm with no bones, slithered out from Total Dark's tall shadow. It wrapped around a hammer on Dr. Barnes' workbench nearby, completely covering it in inky blackness. The tool vanished, and in its place, Total Dark's shadowy arm formed the size and shape of the hammer.

"Interesting," Dr. Barnes said. The hammer arm grew suddenly, many times the size of an ordinary hammer. Total Dark raised it up and the doctor jumped to the floor. Just in time, too; the hammer arm swung down and shattered the computer into a thousand pieces.

"Hey, now that was just uncalled for!" Dr. Barnes scolded the shadow creature.

"*I have a new plan,*" Total Dark hissed. "*You will build me another portal, and it will be much larger this time. Then ALL of my minions can enter this world, and we will conquer it!*"

Dr. Barnes slowly stood up from the floor and dusted off his white lab coat. "There's only one problem with that. There's nothing you can say or do that will make me help you. I'm not afraid of you."

Total Dark swooped toward Dr. Barnes until he was only a few inches from his face. The shadow had no nose, but he made a noise like a dog sniffing the ground.

"*You're right,*" said Total Dark. "*You're not afraid of me. But... you are afraid of something.*" The shadow took a good, long sniff. "*You're afraid for your child's safety. If you don't help me build my portal, the Dark will find your son and bring him to me."*

Dr. Barnes gulped. "You don't leave me much of a choice, Mr. Dark. I guess I'll get started by cleaning up your mess." The doctor kneeled and began picking up pieces of his broken computer. "I hope you're safe, Timmy," he said quietly to himself. "Wherever you are."

CHAPTER 6:

LOST SIGNAL

There was some argument among the bears about the best way for them to get out of the house. The green bear, whose name was Bruiser, wanted to charge for the front door and fight off anyone who got in their way (though Timmy could not imagine Ms. Gertrude fighting off five small, armored bears). Sneak, the orange bear, also wanted to go out the front door, but he wanted to scout ahead and make sure the coast was clear first.

"No way, *Squeak*," said Bruiser. "My way is much better!"

"My name is Sneak!" Sneak insisted. "Sneak, not Squeak! How would you like it if I called you Loser?" He looked around, waiting for someone else to laugh. "Get it? Rhymes with Bruiser?"

"I thought it was funny," said the yellow bear.

"You think everything is funny, Patch," said Bruiser.

"That's quite enough!" Mother scolded. "We'll go out the window and down the fire escape. Understood?"

"Yes, Mother," said Sneak and Bruiser at the same time.

"Wait!" Timmy said. "I need to leave a note

for Ms. Gertrude. I don't want her to worry." Actually, Timmy couldn't imagine Ms. Gertrude worrying about him, but as his nanny it was her job to make sure that he didn't run off into the city with five stuffed bears.

"Okay," said Mother, "but you can't tell her where we're going."

"I don't even know where we're going," Timmy said. He took a piece of notebook paper and a pencil and wrote a note:

Dear Ms. Gertrude,

I'm sorry but I had to leave. I'm safe and I'm going to find my dad.

Timmy

He folded the note in half, wrote Ms. Gertrude's name on it, and put it on his desk. Then he grabbed a backpack and stuffed a few things into it—a change of clothes, a sweatshirt in case it got cold, a notebook and pen, and his house keys.

"Alright," he said. "I'm ready."

Mother opened the window and let the other four bears out first, followed by Timmy, and then her. She warned everyone to be extra silent as they climbed down the fire escape. As he tiptoed down each metal step, Timmy tried to wrap his head around all this but it was difficult to understand everything that was going on around him.

His father had built these five bears to be his guardians against… something. But what that something was, he didn't know. And they were taking him somewhere to meet his father. Why couldn't his dad just come home and get him?

And what exactly were these bears, anyway? It didn't feel right to call them robots; they each had their own personality and they could walk and talk. They were too alive to be called robots. The green bear, Bruiser, obviously liked to fight. The orange one, Sneak, seemed to be some kind of scout (though Timmy didn't know how sneaky he could be when he randomly made those half-hiccup, half-sneeze noises). He heard Bruiser call the yellow one Patch. He didn't get the name of the blue bear, who was mostly quiet so far, so in Timmy's mind he just called him Blue.

And then there was Mother. How strange it was to call a stuffed bear Mother. But then again, she was the leader, and she was warm and nurturing. Timmy's own mom, his real mother, had passed away four years ago when he was only six—right before he and his dad moved the first time.

Timmy missed his mother dearly, but he could still remember her face, and her smile, and the way her brown hair looked red if the sunlight hit it just right. If he closed his eyes and concentrated very hard, he could remember the sound of her laugh and the scent of her perfume.

He hadn't called anyone "mother" in four years, and now he was saying it to a stuffed bear in high-tech armor. Life was really weird sometimes. And right now, Timmy had a lot more questions than answers.

They reached the street safely and silently, Mother helping Timmy down the last few steps. "Alright, Bear Company," she said quietly, "we're heading east. Let's get out of the city and—"

"Wait, wait," Timmy interrupted. He knew it was very rude to interrupt a person when they were speaking, especially adults, but he wasn't sure how rude it was to interrupt a toy. "What do you mean we have to leave the city? My dad isn't in the city?"

"Oh, Timmy," Mother said, "I'm sorry. I thought you knew."

Timmy looked from bear to bear, but no one looked back at him. They all looked at the ground, or the sky, or pretended there was something very interesting about the nearby sewer grate. "Knew what?"

"Come with me," Mother told him. "We should get off the street before we're seen." She led Timmy and the rest of Bear Company to a nearby alley, where Sneak stood watch to make sure no one was coming. The alley was dark, and if Timmy was alone he would have thought it was scary, but being with five armored bears is comforting in the darkest of alleys; besides, their glowing eyes helped, like ten tiny flashlights in the night.

"Timmy," Mother said, "your father is not in

the city. The people that hired him to come here lied to him. They've taken him away to…" She turned to the blue bear. "Keylogger, where was the last transmission from Dr. Barnes?"

"The Arctic," answered the blue bear.

"The Arctic?" Timmy repeated. He wasn't sure exactly where the Arctic was, but he knew it was a very cold, very frozen place that was likely very far from the city. "How do we get there?"

"We don't," Mother said. "Your father had a plan to escape. Our goal is to bring you to a rendezvous point halfway. He'll meet us there."

"A what point?"

"A rendezvous point." Timmy was a smart kid, but he'd never heard the word ron-day-voo before. "It means the place where two people meet," Mother explained.

"Oh." He wondered why she didn't just say

that. It seemed easier. "So we have to go halfway to the Arctic?"

"That's right. I won't lie to you; it's going to be a very long journey, and we don't know what we're going to run into. But we'll have help along the way, and you'll always have us."

Just then, the blue bear, whose name was apparently Keylogger, perked up and said, "Incoming message!" His metal ears in their blue armor twitched left and right, like an antenna trying to pick up a radio signal. "It's from Dr. Barnes!"

"What is it?" Mother asked.

"Just one word: flashers." The blue bear's ears stopped twitching. "That's all. I lost the signal."

"What does that mean?" Timmy asked. "Why did you lose the signal?" He hoped nothing bad had happened to his dad.

"Don't worry, Timmy," Mother said, putting her hand on his arm. "It probably means he was able to escape."

"But what does 'flashers' mean?" he asked.

Bruiser, the green bear, pounded one of his tiny fists against the other and said, "It means we get weapons!"

"It means we have to get to your dad's secret cache," Mother answered.

"Cash?" Timmy didn't understand what money had to do with anything.

"Not cash; *cache*. Cache means a hidden storage place. Your dad has lots of them, all over the world. There's one here in the city, and I bet we'll find flashers there." Mother turned to the orange bear. "What does it look like out there, Sneak?"

Sneak shook his head. "Not good. This city really never sleeps. It might be nighttime, but there are still enough people for us to be seen. We can't just walk down the street, you know."

Mother put one hand on her chin, thinking. "Keylogger, do you know any other way to get around without being seen?"

The blue bear shrugged. "If I had a schematic of the city, I could find us a way. But I would need to get to a computer first."

"There are computers at the public library," Timmy said. "It's only two blocks from here."

"Smart thinking, Timmy," said Mother. "Alright, Bear Company. To the library—and let's not get spotted!"

CHAPTER 7:

OUT OF THE TRASH CAN, INTO THE SEWER

Sneak was right; there were still plenty of people out in the city, even though it was the middle of the night. Timmy had never even been up this late, let alone out walking the streets.

"How can we get to the library without being seen?" asked Patch, the yellow bear.

"I bet I could sneak there," said Sneak.

"Yeah, right," Bruiser replied. "You would

get halfway there and start squeaking!"

"Do I have to separate you two?" Mother warned.

Timmy ignored the bickering bears. He was too busy looking around for anything in the alley they could use to hide the bears from sight. "Aha!" he said loudly. Further down the alley was a side door to a restaurant, and next to that door was a tall plastic garbage can with two wheels. "I have an idea!"

A few minutes later, Timmy rolled the garbage can behind him onto the street. He tried to look straight ahead at the sidewalk and not stop to talk to any strangers. He was sure that the people passing by him were wondering why a ten-year-old boy was out in the middle of the night, dragging a garbage can behind him, but nobody stopped to ask him.

Inside the garbage can were the five grumpy

bears—grumpy because even though they took the garbage out of the can first, it still smelled pretty bad in there.

"Ugh," said Bruiser, "it smells like old cheese in here."

"I'm cramped!" Sneak protested. "Bruiser, get your foot off my head."

"Shh," Timmy said. "Someone will hear you!"

"Hey guys," said Patch. "How many tickles does it take to make an octopus laugh?"

"Not now, Patch," said Mother.

"Ten tickles! Get it? Sounds like tentacles?"

The bears all groaned from inside the trash can.

"Sorry! I tell jokes when I'm nervous!" said Patch.

"You tell *bad* jokes when you're nervous," Bruiser corrected her.

It only took a few minutes for Timmy to roll the trash can the two blocks to the library. But when they arrived, the windows were dark and the door was locked.

"It's closed!" Timmy said. "I should've thought of that."

"It's okay," Mother said from inside the trash can. "Is there a back door?"

Timmy dragged the garbage can around to the back of the building and, sure enough, he found a back door there.

"There's no one around," he said. "You can come out."

The lid of the garbage can sprang open and the members of Bear Company climbed out quickly.

"Oh, fresh air!" Sneak exclaimed.

"How do we get inside?" Timmy asked.

"I'll break a window!" Bruiser offered.

"No," Mother said. "Sneak, see if you can pick the lock. Then Keylogger will go inside. Timmy, you'll go with him and show him where the computers are. The rest of us will stand guard out here."

Sneak hurried over to the door. "As Bear Company's scout, I'm an expert at picking locks," he told Timmy. He held up one of his black robotic fists, and out of the shining orange wrist guard sprang two long, narrow tools. "Look, I'm like a Swiss Army Bear!" He stuck the long picks into the door lock and jiggled them left, and then right, and then up and down.

"Make it fast, Sneak," Mother warned. "It's not good for us to be out in the open like this."

"Almost… there…" Sneak twisted the picks left again, and then right again. *Click!* The lock turned and the back door to the library swung open. "See? Nothing to it!"

"Let's go," said Keylogger. He disappeared through the doorway and into the darkness. Timmy followed, walking carefully with his arms out in front of him. It was very dark inside, and he was afraid that he might trip or run into something.

"Keylogger!" he said in a hoarse whisper. "Where did you go?"

Suddenly he saw two bright blue eyes in the dark ahead of him. "Follow the light," he said. "I can see in the dark."

Timmy followed the two blue lights until he reached the bear. "The computers should be over this way," he pointed. Timmy had spent a lot of time in this library, checking out and returning science-fiction books.

Keylogger climbed up on the chair of the first computer and turned it on. The sudden brightness of the screen made Timmy squint.

Then the blue bear held up his left hand, just like Sneak had done outside, but instead of a lock pick springing out from his wrist guard, he pulled a long white cable from it and plugged it into the computer.

"Ah, I get it," Timmy said. "Your name is Keylogger because you're a computer expert, right?"

"That's right," said Keylogger. "I can hack into just about any computer in the world." The bear didn't even have to touch the keyboard; the screen jumped to life and began showing him a map of the city. "Now I just have to download this to my memory…"

"I have to admit," Timmy said sheepishly, "I've just been calling you Blue in my head."

"Blue," Keylogger repeated. "I like it. You can keep calling me Blue if you want." He unplugged his cord from the computer and it disappeared back into his wrist with a sound like someone slurping a spaghetti noodle. "All done. Looks like we're going to—"

Blue didn't get to finish his sentence, because a gruff voice called out from the dark behind them. "Who's there?" the voice demanded. "I know you're in here!"

"It must be a security guard!" Timmy whispered. "Come on, we have to hide!" Timmy grabbed Blue by the hand and pulled him behind the nearest bookshelf. Just in time, too; the beam of a flashlight swept over the computer desk an instant later. A chubby man in a black security guard uniform frowned as he shined his flashlight left and right.

"Blue, your eyes!" Timmy said. The glowing blue lenses over the bear's eyes were way too bright. "Can you turn them off?"

"I don't think I can!" Blue said.

"Aha!" the security guard cried out. "I see you there, with the blue eyes! Come out right now!"

"*HI-YA!*" Bruiser shouted as he jumped onto the security guard's back. "Run for it, Timmy!" the green bear shouted. "I'll take care of this guy!"

"Hey, get this thing off me!" The guard dropped his flashlight and reached behind him with both hands, trying to pry the bear off of his back.

"Run for it!" Blue shouted. He ran ahead, lighting the way in the dark. Timmy followed as quickly as he could while still being careful not to run into anything. Behind him, he could hear the guard grunting as he struggled against Bruiser.

Outside, Blue and Timmy joined Mother, Sneak, and Patch. "What happened?" Mother asked. "Where's Bruiser?"

They didn't have to answer her question, because a moment later the security guard stumbled out of the back door, still trying to get Bruiser off his back.

"Come on, get off!" the guard shouted.

"Not until you surrender!" Bruiser laughed and put his hands over the guard's eyes. The man wobbled and lurched forward. Bruiser jumped off his back, and at the same time the guard tipped over and fell headfirst into the garbage can.

"Ugh, it smells like old cheese in here!" the guard yelled, his short legs kicking in the air.

"Time to go!" Mother said.

"This way!" Blue led them away from the library. With their garbage can being used by the guard, there was no way for them to hide, so instead they simply ran for it. A few people passing by stopped to stare at the five armored bears dashing past them, each barely coming up to knee-level. But then the people rubbed their eyes, as if they couldn't believe what they were seeing, and the bears were gone just as quickly.

Blue led them into another alleyway. "Down here!"

"This is a dead-end!" Patch said. "There's no way out!"

"Sure there is. Look!" Blue pointed to a sewer grate. The opening was just narrow enough that Timmy and the bears would be able to squeeze through if they laid on their bellies.

"The sewer?" Bruiser complained. "And I thought that trash can smelled bad."

CHAPTER 8:

AFRAID OF THE DARK

Dr. Barnes was alone in the big, wide room of the underground facility. Total Dark had left, likely to see how the takeover of the secret lab was going. The doctor picked up the pieces of the computer that the shadow had shattered. He hoped that he could fix it enough to send a message out to Corps Command, but unfortunately the computer was broken beyond repair.

He worried about what would happen if the Dark managed to take control of this place. The agents told him that there were other experiments going on—what if the Dark gained some super-secret government weapon?

Even more than that, he worried about Timmy. He hoped that his activate command had gone through and that his son was safe with Bear Company. Dr. Barnes wished he could get a message out to General Leo, but without the computer, he had no way to do so.

The door to the lab opened and a young man stumbled inside. He looked very frightened, and he wore a white lab coat, which meant that he was a scientist and not an agent. A tall shadow swept into the room after him—Total Dark.

"*Dr. Barnes,*" Total Dark hissed, "*I have brought you an assistant.*"

"I don't need an assistant," said Dr. Barnes. "No offense," he said to the young scientist.

"With an assistant, you can build faster."

"I'm not going to build anything for you," the doctor said bravely.

"Oh, but you will. Or we will find your son."

Dr. Barnes decided to call his bluff—which means that the doctor decided to try to catch Total Dark in a lie. "I don't think you know who my son is, or where to find him."

The edges of Total Dark's shadow flickered back and forth as he made a horrible grating noise, like nails on a chalkboard.

"Is that... a laugh?" Dr. Barnes asked. "Is that the sound you make when you laugh? Because laughter is supposed to sound pleasant."

"Indeed, doctor, I am laughing. You see, the Dark has taken control of this base. And while you might not be afraid of me, the others here

are VERY afraid of me. They told me all about you, and your son Timmy, and where we can find him."

"Oh, no," the doctor whispered. Those agents! The same people that took him away from the city were now giving the Dark all the information they would need. *What else have they told him?* Dr. Barnes wondered.

"*Now, Doctor, let me introduce you to one of my commanders,*" Total Dark said with a hiss. A second shadow swooped into the room, across the floor, and up the wall—all in an instant. It was so fast it was almost impossible to see it move. Finally the shadow came to a rest next to Total Dark. It was much smaller—no bigger than a human child, in fact—and its shadow flickered across the floor as if it was wearing a billowing cape.

"*This is Shroud,*" Total Dark said. "*And*

I have given him the task of finding your son, Timmy. Shroud, you will take a dozen minions and go into the city. Find the boy and bring him here."

Shroud did not say anything, but swooped out of the lab just as quickly as he'd entered.

"And what will you do with my son when you have him here?" Dr. Barnes asked.

"Nothing... as long as you build the portal," said Total Dark. *"But if you refuse, I will turn little Timmy into a minion of the Dark!"*

"Alright," Dr. Barnes said. "I'll build you a portal. Just please, don't hurt Timmy."

"Good," hissed Total Dark. *"Get started."* The tall shadow swept out of the room, leaving the frightened younger scientist there.

"What's your name?" Dr. Barnes asked him.

"Uh... my name is Arjun, sir."

"Alright, Arjun. What do you know about

quantum mechanics? String theory? Alternate dimensions? The space-time continuum?"

"Oh, I know lots, sir," said Arjun. "I was top of my class at university. The agents kidnapped me because I wrote a paper about parallel universes."

"Good," Dr. Barnes said. "Then let's begin by taking apart the portal and saving whatever parts we can reuse."

"So… you are really going to build him a portal to his world?" Arjun asked. "I know they are threatening your son, but that still seems like a very bad idea."

Dr. Barnes grinned. "Arjun, weren't you listening? I told him I would build *a* portal. I didn't say I would build one back to his world."

Arjun looked confused. "Then where will this new portal lead?"

"Our new portal will lead somewhere safe,"

the doctor told him. "And we'll use it to escape this underground prison. Come on; we have a lot of work to do, and very little time."

CHAPTER 9:

THE SECRET CACHE

If anyone had been walking near the intersection of Tenth Street and Washington Avenue late at night, they might have been very surprised to see what looked like a small bear with glowing orange eyes and orange armor climb out of the sewer grate on the corner. They probably would have stopped to stare, or maybe try to take a picture. And then they would be equally surprised to see another bear, this one green, climb out after the orange bear. And if they weren't yet surprised, they certainly would be when they heard the green bear say, "Well, that was disgusting."

Lucky for Bear Company, no one was around when they made their way out of the sewer and onto the street. Timmy climbed out next, pushing his backpack out first and then shimmying through the grate on his stomach. He was very glad that he brought a change of clothes, because his shirt and pants were now filthy and his shoes were soaked.

Patch came next, who had told no fewer than three very unfunny jokes while in the sewer, followed by Blue and then Mother.

"Keylogger, how much further?" she asked. "We can't stand out in the open like this."

"Actually," said Blue, "we're here." He

pointed across the street to a tall chain-link fence. Behind it was rows and rows of squat rectangular buildings, and each building had dozens of orange sliding doors that looked very much like a garage.

Timmy frowned. "A storage unit?" he asked. "My dad's top-secret hidden cache is a storage unit? That's not very secret at all!"

"Well, it's not the cache that's secret and hidden," Mother admitted. "It's what inside."

The five bears and Timmy dashed across the street to the fence. Halfway there, Patch said, "Hey Timmy. How many bears does it take to screw in a light bulb?"

"No more jokes, Patch," Mother scolded. "It's time to focus." She looked up at the chain-link fence. It was about eight feet tall, which is very tall for a two-foot bear. "Now, how do we get in?"

"I can sneak over the fence and open it from the inside," said Sneak.

"I'll tear a hole in the fence with my bare paws!" Bruiser offered.

"We can use that gate over there," Timmy said simply. "Look, it's not locked."

"Oh," said Bruiser, disappointed. "Sure, I guess we can do that."

Once they were inside the fence, Mother said, "Okay, we're looking for unit seventeen."

"Seventeen? That's my dad's favorite prime number," Timmy remarked.

"That's right," Mother said. Timmy could hear a smile in her voice behind her metallic bear helmet. "I think you're going to find that a lot of little things that you thought might not be important actually are."

"What are we waiting for?" Bruiser said impatiently. "Let's go!"

"Wait!" said Blue suddenly. His metallic ears twitched left and right. "I'm getting an incoming radio call!"

"Is it my dad?" Timmy asked excitedly.

"No... I'm sorry," Blue said. "It's the general."

"The general!" Mother exclaimed. "That means that Corps Command has been activated too!"

Blue's ears stopped twitching, and he held up his right hand. There in the center of his palm was a small black speaker.

"Hello? Hello? Is this thing on?" said a deep voice with a slight growl to it.

"Yes, General! We can hear you!" Mother said into the speaker-paw. "Bear Company has been activated!"

"We have all been activated," said the general. "The entire Corps. Do you have the package?"

"We do," Mother told him.

"Am I the package?" Timmy asked, but no one answered.

"And are you en route?" the general asked.

"That means 'on the way,'" Patch said to Timmy, even though he knew what "en route" meant.

"We will be soon," Mother said. "The doctor's last message was 'flashers.' We're getting them now."

"What are flashers?" Timmy asked.

Bruiser rubbed his hands together. "Weapons," he said.

"Flashers, huh?" the general said through the speaker. "That can't be good. Well, get out of the city as soon as you can. I'll be at the rendezvous point with the rest of Corps Command waiting for Timmy's father to arrive. Radio in if you have anything to report. And be careful, Bear Company!" The speaker crackled once more and then fell silent.

"What did he mean, 'the entire Corps'?" Timmy asked. "Are there more like you?"

"Oh, loads more," Patch replied.

"Bear Company is just a small part of the Corps," said Mother. Then she added, "But we're the best."

"And the smartest," said Blue.

"And the sneakiest," Sneak added.

"And the fiercest!" Bruiser exclaimed.

"Oh, and we're the funniest," Patch chimed in.

Timmy wasn't sure about that last part, but he hoped the rest was true.

Bear Company made their way to unit seventeen, which was at the far end of a row that held units eleven through eighteen. The five bears and Timmy stood outside the tall, orange metal door, which was locked with a padlock.

"Sneak, can you get that open?" Mother asked.

"Hmm…" said Sneak, inspecting the lock. "No, I don't think I can. See, this is a combination lock. It opens by turning these dials to make a series of four numbers. There's no key, so there's nothing for me to pick."

"We could be here all night trying to figure out the combination!" Patch cried. "Mother, what are we going to do?"

"I'll tell you what we're going to do." Bruiser flexed his arms (which was quite funny to Timmy, since he knew that under that green armor, Bruiser was just as soft and plushy as the other bears). "I'm going to tear that lock off with my bare paws!"

Bruiser grabbed the combination lock with

both hands and pulled on it. Naturally, it did not break or even budge. He grunted, twisted, pulled, and yanked, but the lock would not open. Timmy doubted there was anyone who could break a lock with their bare hands, let alone a two-foot-tall bear with an attitude problem.

"Give it a rest, Bruiser," said Mother. "Timmy, I need you to think very hard. Is there any combination of four numbers that your father might have made the code to open this lock?"

Timmy thought about it, and then shook his head slowly. "I can't think of any."

"Think *real* hard," said Blue. "Your father knew that you might have to come here someday, so whatever the code is, it must be something that you would both think of."

"Do you have a lucky number?" asked Patch.

"Or maybe it's the year you were born," said

Sneak.

"Or the last time your favorite team won a championship!" suggested Bruiser.

"Let him think!" Mother scolded.

Timmy *was* thinking—but not about numbers. He was thinking about his father— or perhaps more importantly, he was thinking about thinking *like* his father. Even though his dad was a scientist, and was very smart, and very thoughtful, there were a lot of times that his dad would make quick decisions based on something that seemed very unimportant—sort of like choosing unit seventeen for his secret cache.

So Timmy decided that he would think the same way. He blurted the very first number that came to his head. "One-nine-four-six."

Patch spun the dials on the combination lock and lined up the numbers one, nine, four and six. Then she tugged on the lock. Lo and behold—

which is a fancy way of saying "hey, look at what just happened!"—the lock popped open.

"Great job, Timmy!" Mother exclaimed. "How did you know it would be one-nine-four-six?"

Timmy shrugged. "It was the first number I could think of." He didn't say it out loud, but one-nine-four-six was the very first place that Timmy and his mom and dad lived, when Timmy was very little. It was 1946 Chestnut Avenue, and his mom would make him repeat it over and over again in case he ever got lost and needed to tell someone where he lived. Timmy couldn't help but wonder how many more little surprises like that he would need to remember on this trip

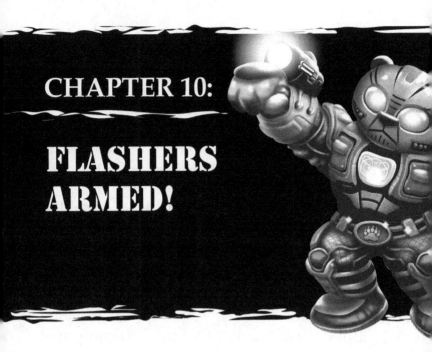

CHAPTER 10:

FLASHERS ARMED!

Once the lock was off, Mother and Bruiser both lifted the door to the storage unit, which rolled up into the ceiling with a sound like thunder. Timmy was worried that someone might hear, but there was no one around this late at night.

Even though it was dark inside, they had the yellow glow of streetlights and ten glowing bear eyes to light up the storage unit. Bruiser was the first one in, bounding ahead, eager to get his paws on some weapons.

"Hey, wait a second!" he almost shouted. "These aren't weapons. This is all junk!"

Timmy looked around. Bruiser was half right; he didn't see any weapons. Instead he saw stacks and stacks of cardboard boxes, old bicycles, and winter coats sealed in plastic bags.

But it wasn't junk. "This stuff," Timmy said in a whisper. "This is my mom's stuff." His dad had kept all of his mother's things—her clothes, her jewelry, everything.

"Now what do we do?" Bruiser complained.

"Quiet down," Mother said. "Dr. Barnes said that this was his secret cache, so the weapons must be in here somewhere. Come on, everyone. Look around."

The five members of Bear Company began

to open boxes and dig around. Timmy wanted to help, but he was still so surprised that his dad was keeping all of his mother's belongings here in the city.

He opened the box closest to him and reached inside. His hands touched something soft and fuzzy—this box was filled with sweaters. He picked one up and held it close to his face.

He could still smell her perfume on it.

"Timmy?" Mother said, putting a hand on his arm. "Are you okay?"

"Yeah," he said. "I think so. I... I thought he got rid of all this stuff."

Mother touched a spot on her neck and her metal helmet slid back from her head with a *zip-zip!* She smiled up at him. "Of course not. Until you came along, your dad loved your mom more than anything. And she loved him. I know that because..."

"Hey, I found something!" Patch shouted. "Mother, look over here!"

Timmy and Mother crowded around the other bears as Patch pushed a cardboard box to the side. Behind a stack of boxes at the back of the unit was a large metal crate. It looked like a very old, very large toolbox; its corners were rusty and there were scuff marks on the top and sides.

"How do we open it?" Timmy asked. He didn't see a lock or a handle or anything on the box.

"Aha!" said Blue. "Look here!" He pointed at a very small rectangular hole on the left side of the crate. "I know what this is." Just like in the library, Blue pulled a white cord from his wrist and plugged the end of it into the rectangle. It fit perfectly.

Suddenly there was a whining noise from

inside the box. Timmy, Patch and Sneak all stepped back, afraid of what might happen. Bruiser stepped closer, ready for anything.

The whining sound became a steady hum, and all of a sudden the top of the crate sprang open, startling everyone. Then the front of the box fell forward, and three drawers inside rose up from the top.

Bruiser did a little dance, bouncing from foot to foot. "Weapons!"

He was right. Each of the three drawers contained all sorts of odd-looking and very high-tech gadgets. They didn't quite look like any weapons that Timmy knew of, but Bear Company seemed to know what they were.

Bruiser was like a kid in a candy store. He quickly began plucking up weapon after weapon. "I want this, and I want this, and—ooh!

I definitely want *this* one."

"No, Bruiser." Mother stopped him. "Dr. Barnes said 'flashers.' That's all we need, and that's all we're taking."

Timmy couldn't see Bruiser's face behind his metal helmet, but he imagined the bear was probably pouting.

"Fine," the green bear said with a sigh.

"Um, Mother… what's a flasher?" Timmy asked.

Mother reached into the bottom drawer and picked up a device that looked sort of like a stubby flashlight attached to a bracelet. "This," she said, "is a flasher." She fitted the bracelet over her wrist so that the flasher was mounted on the back of her arm. "It's a very special type of weapon that your dad invented."

"What does it do?" he asked.

"It's a light cannon," said Blue. "That means

it shoots light."

"Light?" Timmy was confused. When they said "weapons" he thought they meant something like laser guns from a science-fiction book. "What is that going to do?"

"Whatever we're fighting," said Mother, "it's not from this world. It's from… somewhere else. Your dad must know that the flashers are the best weapon against it."

Not from this world? Timmy thought. *There must be a lot that Mother knows, but doesn't want to tell me.*

After each bear had attached a light cannon to their arm, Mother held out a sixth one to Timmy. "Here, put this over your wrist, like this." The bracelet made a quick sucking sound, like *zooop*, and tightened snugly around his arm.

"How does it work?" he asked.

"I'll show you." She pointed to a dial on

the side of the flasher. "There are three settings: cone, burst, and beam. The cone is a very wide, very quick flash of light. The burst is like a strobe light—several small pinpoints that shoot fast, one after another. The beam needs to charge first; you'll hear it whir for a few seconds, and then it will shoot a single straight beam at whatever is in front of you. Now listen, because this next part is very important. You cannot charge the beam for too long. Only a few seconds at a time. If you charge it any longer, it can become dangerous."

"Dangerous? How?" Timmy asked.

Bruiser looked over at him and said one word. "Boom."

Mother nodded. "So do not charge the beam for too long, okay?"

"Okay," said Timmy.

"The flasher will shoot from the movement

of your arm," Mother explained. "All you have to do is give your arm a little flick. Go ahead. Give it a try." She stood back a few feet.

Timmy raised his arm up and pointed it out the door of the storage unit. He turned the little dial to "beam." Right away the flasher made the whirring noise, just like Mother said.

Whhhiiiirrrrr...

After three seconds, Timmy flicked his arm a little bit.

Shoom!

A beam of bright blue light, about as big and round as a quarter, shot from the end of the light cannon and struck the concrete side of the storage building. It lasted for just a few seconds, and then the beam vanished.

"Wow," Timmy said in a whisper. "That was so cool!" He squinted his eyes in the dark to see what the light cannon did to the concrete—but there was nothing, not even a mark.

"It's just a beam of light," said Sneak. "It doesn't hurt or damage real objects, and it won't hurt us."

"Cool," said Timmy. He'd never seen anything like it before—and he was extra glad that he wouldn't be able to accidentally hurt anyone.

Patch closed up the weapons crate and pushed the cardboard boxes in front of it again. Timmy looked one more time at the storage unit full of his mother's stuff.

"Hey Timmy," said Bruiser, "help me close this door." The little bear was too short to reach high enough to pull the door down.

"Wait!" Sneak said suddenly. His mechanical ears twitched left and right, just like Blue's did when he received a radio signal. "I hear something."

"What is it, Sneak?" asked Mother.

Sneak slowly turned the dial on his flasher to "burst."

"Bear Company," he said, "I don't think we're alone here."

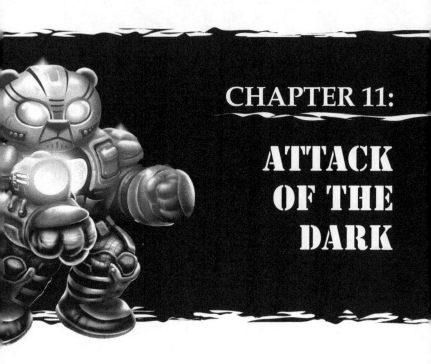

CHAPTER 11:

ATTACK OF THE DARK

"**W**hat is it Sneak? What do you hear?" Mother asked urgently.

"It's a… rustling of some sort," Sneak said quietly.

"Is it a person?" asked Patch.

"No. This is something else," Sneak answered.

"Alright. Everyone, set flashers to burst,"

Mother told them. "Bear Company, form up!"

The five bears formed a circle around Timmy, each with their flashers pointed out. Everyone stayed perfectly still and silent, waiting.

Timmy squinted in the darkness to try to see what was coming. Even with the glow of the nearby streetlights, there were a lot of shadows. But in those shadows, he thought he could see something moving. Or maybe it was just his mind playing tricks on him.

No—something was definitely moving. And some of the shadows suddenly looked a lot darker than others. Impossibly black, like ink. The shadows formed the rough shape of people, with heads and shoulders and long, shadowy bodies. Timmy couldn't see anyone around that could have been casting such a shadow, but it looked like they were surrounded on all sides.

"*Are you afraid of the Dark?*" hissed a

horrible voice from somewhere close by. Even though it was springtime and warm outside, Timmy shivered a little.

"No, we're not," said Mother.

"*You should be.*"

"Who are you?" she demanded.

"*I am called Shroud.*" Timmy couldn't tell exactly where the voice was coming from, but there was one inky dark shape that was taller than the others, the end of its shadow flickering like a cape. "*We serve the master, Total Dark.*"

"The Dark," said Patch in a whisper.

"Well, now we know why we needed the flashers," said Blue.

"Finally!" Bruiser said happily. "Something to fight!"

"Stay in formation, Bruiser," Mother warned. "Our mission is to protect Timmy."

Suddenly the shadow that called itself

Shroud flickered and vanished right before their eyes. Timmy spun around, looking for it; it was behind them. It moved so fast he could barely see it.

"*Give me the boy. We don't need to hurt you,*" said Shroud.

"*But we might anyway,*" said one of the other shadows.

The Dark laughed, a truly terrible noise that sounded like scraping two pieces of sandpaper together.

"We'll never let you take this boy," Mother said. "Bear Company—fire!"

All five flashers fired at once, small balls of blue light bursting from the cannons in every direction. The sky lit up like lightning. The one called Shroud flickered and vanished again, moving out of the way. The flasher burst struck the Dark behind him and it screeched in pain.

"Direct hit!" Bruiser cried out. "Haha!" He tucked into a roll and fired again, hitting another shadow. The balls of light punched small holes in the shadows, who swooped and dodged and retreated.

Timmy stood frozen to the spot. He had a flasher, and he wanted to help, but he was too afraid to move. It was just like in his bedroom when the bears first moved and his legs didn't want to work, except now it was his whole body. They were being attacked by shadows that he could barely see. And they wanted to take him away somewhere, probably some place awful. He couldn't think of anything more frightening than being carried away by Shroud.

"Where's the leader?" Mother shouted. "I lost it!"

"It's too fast!" said Sneak. "We can't even

see it—we'll never hit it!"

Timmy looked all around, squinting his eyes to try to find the dark shape of Shroud. He saw a black blur fly by and disappear... inside the storage unit. They had never closed the door.

"It's there, inside the unit!" Timmy pointed.

"We can corner him inside," said Mother. "Bruiser, Sneak, Patch—take care of the smaller ones. Keylogger and Timmy, with me!" She and Blue dashed toward the open doorway. Timmy urged his legs to work, and he followed behind the two bears.

Inside the storage unit, Shroud bounced around from wall to wall, searching for a weapon against the bears.

"*Aha!*" he hissed as he wrapped his shadow around a square mirror, bonding with it in the same way that Total Dark had bonded with the hammer.

Mother turned the dial on her flasher to "beam" and it charged up. *Whhhhiiirrr....* *Shoom!* The beam of blue light shot out of the cannon and looked like it would be a direct hit on Shroud. But right before it reached him, the shadow's surface turned shiny, like glass. The light beam hit the mirror and bounced off.

"A mirror? That's cheating!" Blue shouted. He fired his light cannon at Shroud in a long burst, but the small balls of light just bounced off the shiny surface.

Shroud laughed in his horrible way. *"You can't hurt me! Your silly weapons are useless against—OW!"* Shroud screeched loudly. As the shadow was distracted by the bears, Timmy fired a burst of his flasher at Shroud's unprotected side, punching small holes in the inky darkness.

Shroud flickered and vanished again. His hissing voice shouted, *"Retreat! We'll come back for you, boy!*"

"Bear Company, to me!" Mother said. The five bears quickly formed a line in front of Timmy, their flashers still pointed.

"Are they gone?" Blue asked.

Sneak's ears twitched left and right. "Yes, I think they're gone."

"Is everyone okay?" Mother asked.

"One of them got me," said Bruiser glumly. He showed them a crack in the armor on his belly. "It hit me with a stick! Can you believe that?"

Patch looked closely at the crack. "Hm. Looks like I can patch this up, no problem."

"There's no time right now," said Mother. "We have to move. We need to get Timmy out of the city. There are way too many places for those things to hide and ambush us." She turned to Blue. "Keylogger, you have the map. What's the quickest way out?"

"You're not going to like it," said Blue. "The fastest way is to cut through a junkyard. If we don't, we have to go eight blocks out of our way."

Mother shook her head. "You're right. I don't like it. But if that's the best way, then that's what we'll do. Bear Company—move out!"

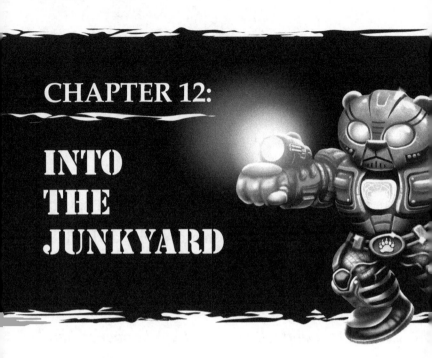

CHAPTER 12:

INTO THE JUNKYARD

"*Well*," said one of Shroud's minions, "*now we know that the light stings.*"

"*And what were those awful-looking creatures with the boy?*" said another minion.

"*I don't like them. They're too... colorful,*" said a third.

Shroud said nothing. He was angry that the Dark had lost the battle and run away to a dark alley. He was even angrier that the boy had hit him. A boy! He would have to be more careful next time. Those weapons of light were dangerous to the Dark.

He looked over his minions. Only one of them was unharmed; all the others had several holes punched in their shadow, like dark Swiss cheese. He pointed to the unhurt minion.

"*You!*" Shroud commanded. "*Go back to Total Dark and tell him what has happened here. Tell him to be careful of the light, and that we will not fail; we will get the boy.*"

The minion quickly swooped out of the alley and away into the night.

"*Shroud,*" said one of the smaller minions, who was missing almost half his shadow. "*We cannot attack again. We are weakened.*"

Shroud moved so fast that even the Dark had trouble seeing him. In a half-second he wrapped himself around the smaller shadow and consumed it. The holes that Timmy had shot in him suddenly filled in; he was whole again.

He turned to his other minions. *"Would anyone else like to tell me that we're weak?"*

"Nope."

"No, sir."

"We're strong. Very strong."

"Good," said Shroud. *"Then come along. We must get to the boy before this thing called 'day' comes."* The Dark swept out of the alley, following behind Shroud.

*　　*　　*

Bear Company moved in a single-file line toward the junkyard: Mother went first, then

Blue, then Timmy, and behind him were Patch, Sneak and Bruiser. Timmy could not help looking all around him as they walked—left and right, up and down—watching the shadows for movement. Once or twice he thought he saw something. His eyes were starting to play tricks on him.

To distract himself from the shadows, he talked to Patch. "So, are you like the doctor or something?" he asked.

"That's right," she said proudly. "I'm the medic of Bear Company. If someone gets hurt, they come to me, and I patch them right up."

"Do you only fix bears?" Timmy asked. "Or can you help people, too?"

"I know everything there is to know about people," she said. "Your dad put every piece of medical knowledge known to man in my head."

"Yeah," said Bruiser, "and every terrible

joke known to man, too."

"Hey, they're not terrible!" Patch said. "Like this one: Why are ghosts bad at lying? Because you can see right through them!"

Patch giggled to herself. Timmy laughed a little, just to be polite. Bruiser was right; it was a really terrible joke.

"You're un-bear-able," Bruiser grunted.

"That's enough joking around," said Mother. "We're here." They stopped at a tall fence with sharp barbed wire at the top. "We can't climb over this. Sneak, can you cut a hole?"

"You bet." Sneak held up his orange wrist and a small pair of wire cutters zipped out from the end. "Give me two minutes."

While Sneak cut a hole in the fence, the rest of Bear Company stayed alert with their eyes on the shadows.

"That was a brave thing you did back there,"

Mother said to Timmy. "You hurt Shroud. He'll think twice about coming after us again."

"Mother, what were those things?" Timmy asked.

She sat in the grass with her back to the fence, and then patted the grass next to her with a hand. "Come, sit with me."

Timmy sat next to her. It felt very good to sit in the cool grass. They had been walking for hours, climbing down fire escapes and through sewers. He hadn't realized how tired he was.

"Your dad is a very smart man," Mother said. "He made a theory, which is just a fancy word for idea, that there are many other worlds that exist at the same time as ours. But we can't see them and they can't see us. So your dad built a window."

"A window," Timmy repeated. "So that he could see into these other worlds?"

"That's exactly right," said Mother. "But nothing could come in through that window."

Timmy was almost too afraid to ask, but he forced himself to say, "What did he see through the window?"

Mother shook her head. "He saw a terrible place made of shadow and darkness. And you know the problem with a window—the things on the other side can see through it too. The Dark got a glimpse of our world."

"But how did they get in?" Timmy asked.

"Some very bad people found out about the window. They lied to your dad and told him that there was a very special, very important job here in the city. When you moved here, they took him and they forced him to build a doorway." Mother shook her head sadly. "I don't know any more than that, but I guess the door worked—but not in a good way."

Suddenly Timmy put two and two together, which is a fancy way of saying that he realized two things were connected. "Is that why he built you, and the flashers? Because he knew that the Dark might find a way to get here?"

"That's right," said Mother.

Next Timmy asked the biggest question on his mind. "But what do they want with me?"

Mother did not answer. Instead she reached both hands around his waist and hugged him tightly. "Don't you worry about that," she said. "As long as I'm around, no one is going to take you anywhere."

Timmy still had a lot of questions, but Sneak interrupted them. "We're through," he said.

"Good." Mother stood up and helped Timmy to his feet. "Keylogger, I want you to send a radio message to the general. Tell him we know what we're dealing with. It's the Dark. Everyone in the Corps needs to get their paws on some flashers."

Bear Company and Timmy climbed through the hole in the fence and stared out at the vast, dark junkyard. Before them were huge mounds of twisted metal and broken-down cars and old refrigerators.

"Bear Company," Mother said, "let's get out of this city."

CHAPTER 13:

SILLY BEARS

In the wide room of the underground lab, Dr. Barnes and Arjun were hard at work on a new portal. The first one had taken Dr. Barnes a whole month to build, but this time he had help. He was sure they could build another one in half that time, maybe even less.

Arjun put down his wrench and wiped some sweat from his forehead. "Dr. Barnes?" he said.

"May I ask you a question?"

"Of course, Arjun."

"Why are we building another portal?" asked the young scientist. "What good will it do to go to another world if we cannot get back home?"

"Ah," said Dr. Barnes, "that's the trick. You see, this portal won't take us to another world. Instead, we are going to try to fold space-time back on itself. If my calculations are correct, this portal will take us to another place here on Earth!"

Arjun smiled. "That is very smart, Dr. Barnes. But... where on Earth will it take us?"

"Well, that's the problem." Dr. Barnes frowned. "I'm not really sure."

Arjun thought for a moment and then said, "I hope it takes us to Hawaii. That would be very nice."

The doctor laughed. "You're right. That

would be nice." But in his mind he thought, *I hope it takes us to Timmy.*

Suddenly he felt a shiver up his spine, like someone had opened a window and let a cold breeze in. He turned to see the tall shadow of Total Dark standing silently behind him.

"What do *you* want?" Dr. Barnes asked.

"*One of my minions has returned,*" Total Dark hissed. "*It seems your son has some help.*"

Dr. Barnes grinned. "Bear Company," he said.

"*And weapons made of light?*"

"No, dummy, they're not made of light. They shoot light." Dr. Barnes rolled his eyes. Made of light? That would be ridiculous.

Total Dark growled. He didn't know what a dummy was, but it did not sound like a compliment. "*I bet you think you're quite smart.*"

Dr. Barnes shrugged. "I do have three

doctorates, and I attended school at—"

"*SILENCE!*" Total Dark boomed. Arjun yelped and hid behind a workbench. "*Your silly bears and light weapons will not save your son. Shroud is one of my fastest and fiercest commanders. He will bring the boy here.*"

"Okay," said Dr. Barnes simply.

Total Dark's shadow flickered in anger. "*Okay?! What do you mean, 'okay'?*"

"I mean you can believe whatever you want to believe. I know what those 'silly bears' are capable of," said Dr. Barnes. "You won't win."

Total Dark growled louder until he sounded like a cement mixer. "*Build faster!*" he shrieked, and then he swept quickly out of the room.

Arjun slowly came out of his hiding place. "Doctor, I am very confused. Weapons of light? Silly bears? What does all this mean?"

"Don't you worry, Arjun," said the doctor.

"It means that we're getting out of here, one way or another. Either our portal will work, or help will come. I know it." *And*, he thought, *there are plenty more surprises for the Dark along the way.*

*   *   *

Shroud and his Dark minions gathered just outside the junkyard. He looked closely at the hole that was cut in the fence; it was about two feet high, just enough for one of those armored creatures to fit through.

"*They went this way,*" said Shroud. "*Into this machine graveyard. All of you, move ahead and find them. I will strike when they least expect it.*"

The shadowy minions flew ahead into the junkyard. Only Shroud stayed behind, looking around at all the twisted, pointy, dangerous objects heaped in large piles.

He had an idea.

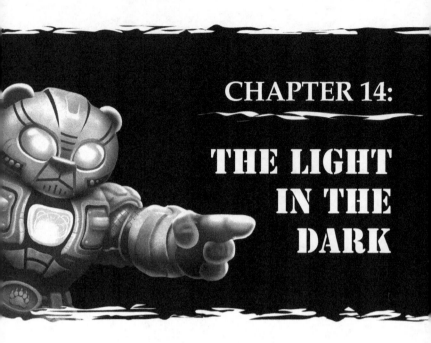

CHAPTER 14:

THE LIGHT IN THE DARK

"Incoming!" shouted Bruiser as the first of the Dark attacked. He lifted his flasher and fired a burst at the shadow.

"Form up!" Mother shouted as the bears surrounded Timmy. They were in the center of the junkyard—they'd come too far to run away and go back now.

All around them the shadows danced and

swooped as the Dark surrounded them. Timmy raised his flasher as well; he was still afraid, but not frozen in fear like he was before. This time, he would help.

"Bear Company, draw them in," said Mother. "Let them get close. Do not fire—not yet." She looked up at Timmy and said, "We still have one more surprise up our sleeve."

"We don't have sleeves," said Patch.

"This is no time for jokes," grumbled Bruiser.

"Who's joking?" Patch asked. "I'm being serious for once."

"Everyone—set your flashers to 'cone,'" said Mother. "Tighten this circle, shoulder to shoulder." The bears formed a very tight circle with Timmy in the center and turned the dials on their light cannons to "cone."

The Dark crept closer, very slowly. They

knew that the light weapons could hurt them, but for some reason the bears weren't using them. Shadows like puddles of tar oozed nearer, forming rough shapes of terrible beasts with claws and teeth.

"Don't be afraid, Timmy," said Mother. "They're just shadows. They're trying to scare us."

"It's sort of working," Timmy said quietly. The Dark closest to him grew shadowy claws as long as knives and long fangs that snapped in the dim moonlight.

"Wait for my signal…" said Mother.

The Dark crept even closer.

"Wait…"

Timmy held his breath.

"Wait…"

The Dark were so close Timmy could almost reach out and touch them.

"NOW!" Mother shouted. Five light cannons fire all at once. A wide cone shot from each one, and with the bears shoulder-to-shoulder, they created a perfect circle of light that shot out from all sides.

The Dark screeched horribly. In an instant, it was over again. The shot was so bright that for several seconds, Timmy couldn't see anything except spots, as if he had just looked directly at the sun.

He rubbed his eyes until the spots went away. When he looked again, the junkyard was still and silent.

"Did it work?" he asked. "Are they gone?"

"I think so," said Blue.

"It did!" Patch shouted. "It worked!"

Bruiser laughed. "I'll tell you one thing. Those Dark might be fast and hard to see, but they ain't so smart. I mean, how dumb do you have to be to—OOMPH!" He didn't get to finish his sentence. Something very fast and very dark struck Bruiser right in the bear-belly and sent him flying into a pile of junk.

"Bruiser!" Timmy shouted.

"Oh, no," said Mother. "It's him—Shroud."

The shadow rose up before them. Shroud looked very different from the last time they saw him. Twisted, spiky metal rose up from his shoulders, from the top of his head, from his flickering tail of a shadow. He had bonded with pieces of scrap from all over the junkyard.

"*This world has so many interesting things to bond with,*" Shroud said, followed by his horrible, grating laugh. "*I think it will be easy to take over, once I get you out of the way.*"

Take over? thought Timmy. So that's what the Dark wanted to do—they wanted to take over the world.

"You have to get through us first!" shouted Sneak. He dialed his flasher to "burst" and fired. The balls of light struck Shroud head-on, but with all the twisted scrap metal covering him, they barely did any damage.

The Dark laughed again. "*You can't hurt me now!*" he said. He swooped toward Sneak and knocked the orange bear aside like he was a fly. Timmy noticed right away that with all the heavy metal covering Shroud, the shadow couldn't move quite as fast—Timmy could see him.

"Patch!" said Mother. "Go help Bruiser! We'll take care of this guy!"

"Right!" Patch dashed away toward the pile of junk where Bruiser had been flung. Timmy followed her, in case she needed help. Mother, Sneak and Blue shot their light cannons at Shroud as he flew around, knocking the bears to the ground easily.

"Bruiser, where are you?" Timmy shouted, searching for any hint of shiny green armor.

"I'm here!" he shouted back. Timmy dug in the junk and found Bruiser wedged between an old microwave and a rusted engine block. His chest armor was very badly cracked.

"Are you okay?" said Timmy. "You look hurt!"

"I'm fine," said Bruiser, "but I can't move my arms. Something must have come loose when he hit me."

"Don't you worry, Bruiser," said Patch. "I'll fix you up quick." She held up her hands. A thin pair of tweezers slid from her left wrist, and a bright blue flame shot from the right—a welding torch. "Cover me while I get him patched up!" she said to Timmy.

He turned to see how the other bears were doing. It wasn't good. Shroud looked like he was playing with them, flinging them this way and that as the balls of light struck nothing but his hard metal shell.

He saw a flash of red as Mother went flying through the air. She got up quickly and ran right back into the fight. But he knew this was hopeless. They couldn't damage Shroud.

"Enough playing around!" the shadow screeched. He swept one shadowy arm and, in one swoop, sent all three bears backwards into an old refrigerator. He slammed the door shut on them and then turned to Timmy.

"Come here, boy," said Shroud. He had no mouth, but if he did, he would be grinning. Timmy fired bursts of his flasher, but the light did almost nothing as Shroud swept quickly over to him. A tendril of black shadow wrapped around Timmy's ankle like a snake, and before he knew what was happening he was on his back, being

dragged away.

"Timmy, no!" shouted Patch.

"Patch, hurry! Fix me!" said Bruiser. "You can't fight him alone!"

"I'm going as fast as I can!" she said, quickly trying to fix the crack on his chest.

The refrigerator door burst open and Mother, Sneak and Blue came tumbling out.

"Timmy!" Mother shouted as Shroud carried him away through the junkyard.

"What do we do?" Blue asked nervously.

Mother shook her head. "There's only one thing to do now. Stand back!" She turned the dial on her flasher to "beam" and it began to charge.

"Mother, no!" shouted Sneak. "It's too much! *Heek!*"

"What's our mission, Sneak?" she asked.

He looked away. "To protect Timmy."

"That's right. So if I don't make it, you

need to get him to the rendezvous point," she commanded. "Now stand back!"

Wwwwwhhhhhhiiiiirrrrr... Her flasher charged up.

Timmy struggled to get loose from Shroud's shadowy grip, but he couldn't. Then he had an idea. He clicked the dial to "beam," let it charge for a few seconds, and then—*shoom!* He fired the beam directly at the dark tendril holding onto him.

Shroud screeched as Timmy shot through the tendril. "*That hurt, boy! Like it or not, you're coming with me!*"

"No, he's not." The leader of Bear Company stood about twenty feet away, her arm raised. Her flasher was making a sound so high-pitched that it hurt Timmy's ears. She was overcharging her beam.

"Mother, no!" he shouted.

"*Ha!*" Shroud laughed. "*Your weapon is useless against me.*"

"We'll see." She fired.

CHAPTER 15:

MOTHER'S SACRIFICE

*S*HHOOOOMMM!

The beam of light that shot from the flasher was so brilliant and white that Timmy had to cover both his eyes. Shroud did not have time to screech or cry out; the shadow evaporated in an instant under the intense beam.

Still covering his eyes, Timmy heard an amazing *BOOM!* so loud and strong that it shook the ground under him.

Then it was quiet.

When he finally uncovered his eyes, all he could see was spots again. It took a full minute before he was able to see anything else. Where Shroud was standing just a minute ago was now just a pile of scrap metal. The shadow was gone.

"Mother!" he shouted, jumping to his feet. "You did it!" He looked around. "Mother?" He didn't see her anywhere. "Oh, no," he whispered.

In the place that Mother was standing a minute ago there was now only a small bit of red fuzz. He bent down and picked it up between his fingers. It felt warm in his hand.

The other four bears gathered around him, their heads bent low.

"Her flasher exploded," Bruiser said quietly.

"She's… gone," said Blue.

"No. She can't be gone." Timmy did not

want to believe that Mother had sacrificed herself to save him. "She can't be gone!"

"I'm sorry, Timmy," said Patch.

"Not… gone," said a voice from nearby.

They all turned as Mother slowly rose to her feet. The blast of her flasher exploding had sent her flying, and her red fur was badly singed in many places.

"Mother!" Timmy ran to her and hugged her tightly. Her plushy body felt warm and familiar. "How did you do that?"

"I… I knew the flasher would explode," she said weakly. "So I… pulled back my armor. My stuffed body absorbed the explosion."

"You shouldn't have done that just to save me," Timmy said.

"I had to," she said.

"Because I'm your mission, right?"

"No, Timmy." She hugged him again.

"You're not just a mission. You're much, much more."

"Mother, let me take a look at you," said Patch.

"I don't think my armor is working." Mother frowned as Patch inspected the metal box on her back.

"Can you fix her?" Timmy asked.

"Hmm…" said Patch. "Looks like you fried something back here. I think I can fix it, but it might take me a while. Maybe a whole day."

"We can't wait that long to get Timmy out of the city," said Mother.

"Maybe we can. Look!" Blue pointed to the sky, which had started to turn a light purple as dawn came. "It's almost morning. We can wait out the day hiding here in the junkyard."

"Yeah, the Dark can't attack during the day… right?" Sneak asked.

"I don't know," said Mother. "But I don't see any other choice. Alright, Bear Company. We'll wait out the day here while Patch tries to fix me up. At night, we get out of here. You can bet the Dark will send more after us."

Timmy slipped the flasher off his wrist and handed it to Mother. "Here," he said.

"But… if you give this to me, you won't have any way to defend yourself against the Dark," she said.

Timmy shrugged. "I'm just a kid. You're an awesome armored fighting bear. I think you could get more use out of it than I will."

"Thank you." She took the flasher and fit it over her plushy wrist. "Don't worry, Timmy. I told you that as long as I'm around, nothing will hurt you, and I mean it. We're going to get you back to your dad, and we're going to defeat the Dark."

"I know we will," said Timmy, and he meant it too.

CHAPTER 16:

REMEMBER MS. GERTRUDE?

Ms. Gertrude awoke and stretched her arms. It was morning; time for another day of pretending to be a nanny. She got up from her bed and dressed and went downstairs to the kitchen. She poured a bowl of cereal, a glass of milk, and put two pieces of bread in the toaster.

Then she stood at the bottom of the stairs and called up. "Timothy! It is time to eat!"

The toast popped, and then got cold. Still, Timmy did not come downstairs.

She called up the stairs again. "Timothy! Time for breakfast!"

Ms. Gertrude waited, listening for the sounds of feet on the floor or running water in the bathroom. She did not hear anything.

"Timothy?" she called up once more. She didn't want to have to go upstairs and wake him. It was so much easier when he came down to her.

She sighed and climbed the stairs to his bedroom. She knocked sharply on the door twice. "Timothy! Are you still sleeping?" It was very odd for the boy to sleep in; he was normally awake quite early.

Ms. Gertrude slowly opened the bedroom door. Right away she noticed that several things were wrong. The first, and most important, was that Timmy was not there. Secondly, the window was open. And lastly, there was a note with her name on it sitting on his desk.

She opened it and read:

Dear Ms. Gertrude,

I'm sorry but I had to leave. I'm safe and I'm going to find my dad.

Timmy

"Oh, that's not good," she mumbled. She quickly left the room, but then she paused. The shelf where Timmy kept his stuffed bears was empty. Why on earth would he bring his toys along? What an odd child.

Downstairs, Ms. Gertrude fetched her purse and dug her hand around in it until she found a small makeup compact, the round kind that had a flip-up mirror inside—except that when she flipped it open, it was not a makeup compact at all, but a well-disguised communicator.

Instead of showing a reflection of her face, the small round mirror instead showed the image of a man in a black suit and black sunglasses.

"This is Gertrude," she said into the device.

"Report," the man on the screen said.

"Timothy Barnes has run away," Ms. Gertrude said. "He left a note saying that he was going to find his father."

"Strange," said the man.

"Yes, I agree. He is a strange boy," said Ms. Gertrude.

"No," said the man, "I mean it's strange because last night, Ice Base Delta was compromised."

"Compromised?" Ms. Gertrude repeated, surprised.

"Yes. It means that it was taken over by

someone—"

"I know what compromised means!" Ms. Gertrude snapped. "Who compromised it?"

"We don't know yet," the man told her. "But if Dr. Barnes was somehow able to get a message to his son it might explain why Timothy Barnes ran off."

"What do you want me to do?" Ms. Gertrude asked.

"Find him, if you can," said the man. "That boy is the only way we can keep Dr. Barnes working."

"Finding missing children is *not* what I joined the agency for," Ms. Gertrude said, annoyed.

"He must have someone helping him if his plan was to get all the way to Ice Base Delta," the man said. "Find the kid, and you'll find whoever Barnes has working on the outside. And if we're lucky, maybe you'll find out who took control of the base."

"Fine," she said. "I'll see what I can do." She snapped the compact communicator shut. Ms. Gertrude groaned. She was hoping to have a nice relaxing day of watching soap operas while Timmy did his schoolwork upstairs in his room. Now she would actually have to put shoes on and go outside.

"I'm coming to find you, Timothy Barnes," she said out loud, to no one in particular. "Right after I eat your breakfast."

**END
OF
BOOK
ONE**

BEAR COMPANY
will return in
DARK CORPS SERIES
BOOK 2

About the Author

Cameron Alexander is the pen name of a mysterious wizard from a different time and a different world. Search for him if you can and if you find him, let me know. He owes me 10 dollars.